This Is Not a Joke...

Malcolm turned the book over in his hands. It took planning, and effort, to print a book like this one. He riffled through the pages. Maybe two hundred pages, or more, of content.

Who the heck had time to do all that as a joke?

Was he on camera? Was that what this was all about?

He looked around nervously. There were a handful of pedestrians approaching, but none of them looked like they were carrying any cameras. No sign of any recording equipment attached to the bridge.

The whole idea seemed silly to him. Who in their right mind would do a reality show about people committing suicide? And how would you identify your participants, anyway?

Still angry, but equally curious now, he opened the book again and read:

> **Are you always this slow?**
>
> **No, this is not a joke. No, this is not a TV reality show. You are not on *Candid Camera* or some demented edition of *Survivor*.**
>
> **I'm a magic book.**
>
> **Get over it, already.**
>
> **Really, this is the most boring part of meeting a new reader.**

Stories by David Keener

Clash by Night (forthcoming)
The Rooftop Game
An Unlikely Hero
The Whispering Voice

Stories in Anthologies

The Curator
Fantastic Defenders
The Forever Inn (forthcoming)
The Outsiders
Reliquary
Second Round
Tranquility and Other Myths

As Editor

Fantastic Defenders
The Forever Inn

AN UNLIKELY HERO

David Keener

Previously published as
The Good Book

Tannhauser Press

An Unlikely Hero

Previously published as *The Good Book* in June 2017.

Published by Tannhauser Press
www.tannhauserpress.com
Fredericksburg, VA 22407

Print ISBN: 978-1-945994-90-6

Packaging by Worlds Enough LLC
Cover Design by Don Anderson
Copyediting by Donna Royston

For my parents. I wish you could have read this.

CONTENTS

THE MAGIC BOOK

EXTRAS

AN UNLIKELY HERO

1. MO{U}RNING WALK

Malcolm Jameson paced methodically through Donahoe Park, a neatly landscaped area about halfway down Mackenzie Hill from where the downtown end of the Hardesty Bridge was anchored. The elevation of the park provided a panoramic view of the entire waterfront and there were park benches placed at strategic lookout points to allow visitors to enjoy the scenery.

Malcolm remembered sitting with Ellen on one of those benches, laughing and joking about the *babymoon* she wanted to plan. She'd found out she was pregnant, and had wanted the two of them to go on a romantic vacation together, almost like a second honeymoon, before the baby arrived.

He'd said his final good-byes to all of them yesterday, at the cemetery. Three marble gravestones, one larger than the other two, draped with flowers and surrounded by fresh, green grass. He missed Ellen. He missed Susan and Billy. A parent should never outlive his children. It was too damn heartbreaking.

He reached the stairs up to the pedestrian sidewalk that ran along one side of the bridge, a major traffic artery for the city, and started climbing. He was a little winded by the time he reached the top, so he leaned against the railing and rested for a moment, just enjoying the view and the light breeze that ruffled his hair. Behind him, he could hear cars passing by on the main roadbed of the bridge.

A group of six women joggers in pastel sweat suits passed him, gossiping excitedly about mundane things, then a few bicyclists whizzed by. People with stuff to live for.

Malcolm pushed himself away from the railing and strolled up the slight slope of the bridge. It took him about ten minutes to reach the center of the span.

He stopped and leaned against the railing one last time, partly to take in the view and partly to plan how he was going to climb over the barrier. He'd envisioned himself doing a proper swan dive, although he wasn't sure why that mattered.

He heard chattering voices nearby as a group of four elderly walkers approached him. He wanted to be alone. He didn't want anybody to be disturbed or horrified, as they might be if they were too close.

He waited for the walkers to pass. There was a bicyclist in yellow and black spandex riding gear coming up behind the women. Once he passed, there was nobody for quite a distance in either direction.

That's when he'd do it.

The geriatric walkers strode past Malcolm without giving him a second glance. All he needed to do now was wait for the cyclist to pass.

Malcolm was surprised when the biker coasted to stop next to him. The man looked to be in his late twenties, with long brown hair that pushed out from under his peaked, yellow helmet. He got off his bike and put down his kickstand. Then he reached into a small canvas pack that was attached to the back of his bike and pulled out a book.

He stepped over to Malcolm and held the book out to him. "Hey, man. This is for you."

"What?"

"This book is gonna change your life, dude. I can feel it in my bones."

Malcolm looked at the paperback that the biker was holding. It had a garishly colored cover that carried the title, "This Book Is Going to Change Your Life." The author was listed as Seymour Subrosa. The cover was battered and creased, and the corners were a little dog-eared, like it had been passed around a lot.

Malcolm couldn't help laughing. He couldn't think of a more incongruous book to hand to somebody who was about to perform a terminal swan dive.

"That's all right," Malcolm said, still chuckling a little. "You keep it. I'm not in the market for a book like that."

"Dude, I'm not leaving until you take the book." The biker was insistent, gazing fixedly at Malcolm's face.

His intensity made Malcolm a little uncomfortable. He had no idea why this guy was being so adamant about him accepting the book.

"All right, all right," he said, intending only to placate the man.

He took the book from the man, who smiled at him, and said, "Live long and prosper."

Great, a mad trekkie. Just what I needed.

The man got back on his bicycle and peddled away, leaving Malcolm holding the book. He supposed he could just put the book down on the sidewalk and then jump. Somebody would probably pick it up.

The book lover in him chafed a little at the idea. That wasn't really how you treated a book. Plus, what would happen to the book if nobody picked it up?

He turned the book over in his hands. The back of the book didn't really say what it was about, except for implying that it was some sort of self-help guide. It featured testimonials from people Malcolm had never heard of. In fact, it was kind of funny, but none of the testimonials seemed to be from anybody famous. On any book he'd ever seen, even if you didn't recognize who was being quoted, there was usually something like "Author of New York Times bestseller, 'Blah blah blah.'"

He flipped to the introduction.

> **The world changes constantly. Every day newspapers and online news sites tell us about new scientific developments, new technologies, new ways of doing business and new social media sites so people can interact in different and supposedly more effective ways. No matter how fast things change, though, there's still one constant.**
>
> **People.**
>
> **You can change the tools and the medium of communication, but we are all still just people. Humans. *Homo sapiens*. We are all possessed of the same feelings and emotional**

apparatus that we've had, as a species, for the last two hundred thousand years.

Well, that hardly seemed promising. Too much boilerplate scientific-speak, obviously designed to emphasize the importance of the self-help message, which would undoubtedly consist of a bunch of totally non-scientific twaddle. He flipped past a few pages without reading them until he came to the heading, "Who This Book is For."

This book is for anybody who's ever felt unsure about their place in the world, or even whether they should stay in it. It's for people who have felt grief so deeply that they've ended up feeling totally disconnected from everyone around them. It's for people like Malcolm Jameson, who lost his wife and children two years ago today in a senseless vehicle accident with an eighteen-wheeler delivery truck for a national grocery store chain.

What the hell? Malcolm slammed the book shut angrily and looked around wildly for that damned biker.

2. FALLING

The bicyclist was nowhere in sight, which was unsurprising since Malcolm had spent several minutes examining the book. If this was some sort of joke, it was a cruel one. He thought about chucking the book off the bridge, but somehow that just seemed wrong.

He snorted in bemusement. Thirty-seven, and here he was, a creature of conditioning. He could no more toss the book into the river than he could just abandon it to the elements when the biker had first given it to him.

He considered the book. What kind of jerk plays a joke on a man about to commit suicide?

More importantly, how had the guy known to give him the book? It wasn't like Malcolm had announced his plans.

In fact, there hadn't even been that much to plan. He'd already had a will in place from well before the Accident. All of his bills were in order, thanks to the settlement. All he had to do was take one long step and his brother would inherit everything. He had no doubts that his oh-so-practical brother would use the money to set up college funds for his nephews and nieces. Arguably, his absence would be beneficial to the rest of his extended family.

He turned the book over in his hands. It took planning, and effort, to print a book like this one. He riffled through the pages. Maybe two hundred pages, or more, of content. Who had time to write that all as a joke? Even if you assume that the biker had lifted the content from somewhere — maybe from the Internet — you still had to customize it, get it ready for publishing, get it printed…and get it delivered from the publisher so you could play your little joke.

Who the heck had time to do all that?

Was he on camera? Was that what this was all about?

He looked around nervously. There were a handful of pedestrians approaching, but none of them looked like they were carrying any sort of video camera. No sign of any obvious cameras attached to any of the bridgework around him.

The whole idea seemed silly to him. Who in their right mind would do a reality show about people committing suicide? And how would you identify your participants, anyway?

Still angry, but equally curious now, he opened the book again, flipped to the same page and continued reading from where he'd left off.

> **Are you always this slow?**
>
> **No, this is not a joke. No, this is not a TV reality show. You are not on** *Candid Camera* **or some demented edition of** *Survivor.*
>
> **I'm a magic book.**
>
> **Get over it, already.**
>
> **Really, this is the most boring part of meeting a new reader.**

What. The. Hell.

This had to be some sort of joke. Anything else was inconceivable. Malcolm looked around again as more pedestrians passed him. Nobody paid any attention to him.

He looked down at the open page and read the next paragraph.

Start walking back to the Sanavale side of the bridge. We've got work to do today. Time waits for no man, nor even magic books.

What was that movie? The one with Michael Douglas where he was rich and powerful, but he secretly wanted to know what could drive a man, like his long-dead father, to commit suicide. Malcolm racked his brain for a moment until the answer popped into his head. The movie had been called *The Game*.

The main character had been ruthlessly manipulated and systematically stripped of everything he valued, until he'd felt he had no choice left but to jump to his death as his father had done. But it had all been a game, with no actual harm to the man.

Was that what this was? Not a joke, but somebody playing a game with him? He looked down again.

This isn't a Hollywood movie. Now, start walking. We're on a tight schedule here.

Malcolm started walking back the way he'd come. He wasn't sure what to think anymore; the book seemed to be addressing him in context with his thoughts, but that was impossible. Could this all be some elaborate psychological experiment?

Well, curiosity had always been one of his weaknesses. He'd play along with this whole charade for now.

He flipped to the next page.

> **Malcolm, you can call it a charade if it makes it easier for you to accept this. But the reality is that we've got serious stuff to do today.**
>
> **Right now, you need to be back in Donahoe Park, over by the big fountain, by exactly 9:03 AM. Not a moment later.**

9:03? Malcolm looked at his watch. He'd have to move a little faster to get there in time. He sped up his steps. He figured he probably looked like one of those power walkers now, the ones that he'd always thought looked so silly.

"What's this about?" Malcolm asked, juggling his conflicting feelings about interacting with the book. It felt more natural to conduct a conversation aloud, but also silly to be talking to an inanimate object. Looking down, he saw that more text had appeared on the page since he'd last glanced at it.

Finally, an intelligent question.

You might say that it's about Good vs. Evil, although that's quite a simplistic view. In another way, it's about entropy, the eventual heat-death of the universe and the intrinsic value of a human life.

"Um, please forgive me, but that doesn't really help me a lot."

If somebody was playing a game with him, it was an extremely sophisticated one. Malcolm had never heard of a technology that could dynamically make print appear on a paper page while the book was being carried in someone's hands. This was far, far beyond any ereader technology he'd ever heard of.

I don't forgive. I'm a book, not a priest.

"I ask a question. You give me an answer that's nonsense."

It could be nonsense. It could simply be an answer to which you haven't given enough thought.

Malcolm trudged down the same stairway that he'd originally climbed to get up to the bridge. Reaching the bottom, he turned right and took the winding trail that led to an ornate fountain occupying the center of a wide circle of asphalt. The exterior of the circle was landscaped with well-trimmed bushes alternating with benches. On one side of the circle, a concrete stairway with metal railings descended from street level a little further up the hill.

Malcolm surveyed the area. Nothing looked out of the ordinary. It was just an intersection in a park where two trails and a stairway met. He examined the book again, but no new text had appeared on the page. He flipped to the next page, and discovered that it was blank.

He looked at his watch. 9:02.

He studied the people around him. By the fountain, there was a young businessman in a suit looking at his smartphone. Coming down the stairway, an old lady carrying a long umbrella that was closed. A twenty-something female jogger approached from one of the trails. Just outside the circle, a middle-aged man was walking an improbably effeminate toy poodle.

That was interesting. To his recollection, rain had not been predicted at all for today, so why was the old woman carrying an umbrella? And, wait, was she actually wearing slippers?

Malcolm headed towards the stairway. He'd almost reached it when the old woman caught her toe on an irregular, cracked section of the step she was on and tumbled into the air with a cry. Malcolm darted forward and caught her before she hit the ground, then exerted himself to bring her safely back to an upright position. She was heavier than she looked.

She screeched, "Rape! Rape!" and began beating him about the shoulders with her umbrella.

He held up his hands to defend himself from her blows and quickly backed away. The other people around the circle turned to watch the unfolding drama. The old woman glared at him, holding the umbrella menacingly in his direction.

"Barbarian scum," she muttered, turning away and marching slowly and defiantly across the circle, exiting past the jogger who had stopped to look at the commotion.

The man with the toy poodle stepped up beside Malcolm. "Some people are easier to help than others."

"Yeah," Malcolm replied.

"Kinda reminds me of my wife."

Malcolm shot him a sideways glance.

3. THE DEAL

As the man and dog walked away, Malcolm took a seat on one of the benches and opened the book again.

> It's true. Some people are easier to help than others.
>
> In this case, her name is Beatrice McDonald and she's no longer all there mentally. She's ninety-three years old, suffers from episodes of dementia and she'll be dead within the year.
>
> For the last sixty-two years, she's been a modestly successful writer of very formulaic and squeaky clean romances, a perfectly reasonable

reaction to the molestation, rape and abuse she suffered as a child and a young woman. Unbeknownst to her family, though, she's been writing a much different book, her magnum opus, for the last forty years.

Thanks to you, she didn't break her hip today, so she won't have to waste her remaining time with medical issues. She'll have enough moments of lucidity to put the finishing touches on her novel. The typed manuscript will be found among her effects by her granddaughter, who will be so moved by the eloquence and raw power of her story that she'll end up self-publishing it on Amazon.com after it's rejected by more than twenty traditional pub-lishers. It will become a viral hit online and ultimately become an inter-national bestseller.

More important than the acclaim, though, is the way that it will strike a chord with women all around the world who are in unhealthy and often disastrous situations. Her book will

change more lives than you can possibly imagine.

Malcolm said, "Was this supposed to convince me not to do my swan dive?"

"No," the book said. "Saving Beatrice was something that needed to be done. You were just handy."

"You used me." Malcolm laughed.

"You let me. Besides, you're too stubborn to give up so easily."

Malcolm looked up from the book. Everything around him looked so normal, and yet, here he was, talking to a book. *Probably better jump before the big men in white suits come to put me away.*

"You know," Malcolm said. "It was weird when you started responding to what I was thinking. But it's really absolutely bizarre watching my words appear before I even have a chance to speak them."

Wondering what the book was going to say next, he read:

"It's faster, though. We've got a lot to do to today, and you've been kind of slow so far."

"Great, so now I'm being insulted by a book."

"The truth is the truth, Malcolm. Deal with it."

"Maybe so, but I don't have to do anything for you."

"True, that's why I'm going to offer you a deal."

"Yeah, right." Malcolm leaned back on the bench. "I thought only the Devil offered deals."

"Souls are overrated as a currency. Plus, the over-the-top symbolism is kind of passé. Do you want to hear the deal or not?"

"I guess."

"All right. You want to end your life, but you're still vain enough to care what people think about you after you're gone, especially your older brother. If you jump, you just know that he'll tell everybody how big a loser you were. That you just couldn't cut it."

That sounded about right. His brother, Jacob, was all about money as the ultimate measuring stick for success. To him, the things you did either made money or incurred an "opportunity cost" in wasted time that would have been better spent doing something that could be monetized.

"So, here's the deal. Be my avatar today. Help me help people, and in exchange you'll be provided with the opportunity to die a heroic death. The kind of death where people will be sad that you're gone, but proud to have known you."

Malcolm thought about it for a moment. There had to be a catch of some kind.

"There's no catch, Malcolm."

"All right. I'll do it."

4. CHOOSE YOUR OWN ADVENTURE

Malcolm spent the rest of the morning walking around the riverfront area performing odd errands for the book. He chased down and caught a yellow Lab puppy, perhaps six months old, which had slipped out of his collar, leaving the seven-year-old girl who'd been walking him distraught.

As he carried the squirming puppy back to the girl, he was struck by how much she looked like his daughter, Susan. Even the blue dress she was wearing reminded him a little of Susan's last Halloween and the light blue Cinderella dress she'd been so excited about. He almost broke down as he helped the little girl get the collar back on her dog.

On Cannery Street, near the cafe where he'd taken Ellen for their first date, he helped a harried mother with five children, with ages like a staircase, carry packages out to her car.

Later, at the urging of a young boy, he climbed a tree in McPherson Square to retrieve a kitten, receiving a nice set of scratches on his right wrist in the process. Ordinarily he might have worried about infection or at least scheduled a tetanus shot, but he wouldn't be around long enough for that to be a concern.

Still a little out of breath from his last exertion, Malcolm sat down on a convenient stone bench near the tree he'd just climbed. McPherson Square was a neatly groomed square about twenty yards wide with a sidewalk fringe, like an island of greenery with concrete beaches in an asphalt sea.

"This is real, isn't it? I mean, us helping people, it's not some pre-arranged game, is it?"

A passing businessman looked oddly at Malcolm talking to himself. Ignoring him, Malcolm once again opened the book.

"Yes, this is real. It's not a game. And the choices you make today are entirely yours to make."

"How do you do this? How do you know about all the things you're telling me?"

"Do you know how you breathe?"

Malcolm thought for a moment. "I understand the process, but I don't really have to think about it."

"It's much the same for me. I know what I need to know when I need to know it. The real difference between us is that I have a purpose, and you're still looking for one. Well, that and I have pages."

Malcolm raised his eyes from the book.

He took exception to the book's characterization of him. There was nobody in his life anymore, just an empty ache where his family used to be. There was no reason to get up each morning just to face another endless and empty day. No reason to stay around. His purpose hadn't changed since earlier this morning, just been delayed by the book's manipulations and, admittedly, his own innate curiosity.

Somewhat frustrated with the book, he decided to ask a more difficult question. "So, are you God?"

Looking down again, he read:

"For those who want to learn, there's a saying that one can never ask a stupid question. The saying is wrong. That's a stupid question. I'm not God. I'm a book. I can communicate thoughts and ideas, but that is all."

"You predict the future."

"Do you think it's going to rain today?"

"No."

"See, you're predicting the future, too.

"I can't predict the things that you're telling me about."

"That's not my fault."

Exasperated, Malcolm closed the book. Maybe there really were magic tomes but, if so, why did he have to get one with an attitude?

He leaned back and watched the pedestrians and the traffic for a few minutes, holding the closed book in his lap. Everybody seemed to have places to go except him. He felt relaxed and at peace. This would all be over for him in a short time, once the book was finished with him.

He looked down at the book's garish cover and considered the inevitable dilemma of anybody who possessed a magic book, assuming that he wasn't in a club all by himself. No matter how irritating it was, if you had a book that could answer any question, how could you ignore it?

He sighed. Then, feeling perverse, he turned the book over and flipped to the last page.

Malcolm flips to the last page of the book in a misguided attempt to see what lies ahead before the book is ready to let go of its revelations. The book, long since wearied of this tactic on the part of its many readers, has evolved a unique strategy to deal with such killjoys.

Malcolm now has a choice to make. He can…

- **Turn to Page 23 to continue the conversation he was having.**

- **Turn to Page 79 to discover the exact date and time of his death. Note that selection of this choice makes this future immutable.**

- **Turn to Page 151 to ask some inane questions while he figures**

out what he really wants to do with the book.

- **Or he may reject his unique knowledge that magic truly exists and simply close the book, leave it on the bench, and go jump off a bridge.**

Malcolm slammed the book shut and stood up. He wasn't sure what he was expecting, but that certainly wasn't it. His own life as a *Choose Your Own Adventure*^{TM} story. He dropped the book unceremoniously on the bench and walked away, almost shaking with rage.

He thought: *On the last day of my life, I shouldn't have to put up with being ridiculed.* And then, *Why not? Was it any worse than what people are going to say when I'm gone?*

He stopped ten paces away from the bench, his mind churning, a whirlwind of thoughts. Reluctantly, he came to the conclusion that the book, however irreverent it might have been, had always taken anything he'd asked anything seriously. It was he who hadn't taken the book seriously.

He was the one who'd still been treating this all as a game.

Malcolm turned and walked back, sat down and picked up the book again. He held it in his hands and hesitated, before he opened it to page 23. He said, "Does God exist?"

"Well, at least that's a better question. One of the big ones, in fact. So I'll answer you this way. What is God? Would you even know him if he showed up?"

"I don't know," Malcolm answered.

"How would an ant describe you? Would it even be able to perceive, let alone understand, a being that much greater than them?"

"Are you saying God is too complicated to understand?"

"I'm just a book. Do you understand me? Completely and totally?"

"No," Malcolm said.

"Here's what you need to know, then. Something like fourteen billion years ago, there was nothing. Then there was a light. A thousand trillion infinities of universes could have come into existence in the Big Bang.

"But we got this one, with physical laws just right to allow matter to form.

With intricate rules that foster emergent properties like life and the rise of intelligence. Look around you. Everything you see is a miracle.

"Do you think this was just an accident?"

Malcolm gazed at the pedestrians scattered all around the square, striking in their diversity, heading for an early lunch or various errands that brought them here at this exact moment in time. There were cars, work trucks and buses; they were moving, turning, changing lanes or stopped at lights. How improbable was it that all this should be here, right now, for him to see?

He shook his head. Maybe it *was* miraculous, but it was kind of ordinary, too. Just another day in the city. An ordinary day.

5. BUS STOP

Malcolm sat on the bench and watched the bustling traffic for a while. Finally, he looked down again at the book.

> **Stop woolgathering. You need to be at the intersection of Lamont and Castle by 11:21. On the corner with the Pizza Hut. Move!**

Struck by the book's urgent tone, Malcolm closed the book, stood and looked at his watch. Six minutes to get to an intersection three blocks away. He moved off at a slow jog.

He had to do some judicious jaywalking to get there in time, but he managed it just barely. He surveyed the intersection curiously. Nothing looked unusual. It was just an intersection with a streetlight and electronic signs to tell pedestrians when it was safe to walk.

He thought about flipping to the next page, but given his last experience, he thought that might be a bad idea.

A small group of pedestrians gathered around him waiting for the "Walk" signal to come on. He studied the people, who looked like any random assortment of office workers that you might see in the city on any given day. The man in the dark suit was probably a lawyer, he decided. Over there, a secretary. An office manager wearing a conservative pantsuit. A frumpy-looking, middle-aged woman carrying a McDonald's bag. A tall, brunette woman with long hair holding a cell phone to her ear and clutching a Starbucks cup in her other hand.

Malcolm's gaze lingered for a moment on the woman with the cell phone. Something about the animated expressions flitting across her face as she talked grabbed his attention. She was wearing a form-fitting but conservative blue dress with a wide black belt that accentuated a trim waist.

She certainly was pretty, Malcolm thought, and then felt instantly guilty. There was only one woman for him, and she was two years gone, now.

The light changed to "Walk" and the tall brunette stepped into the street, not realizing that a big city bus had run the light and was barreling across the intersection. She looked up and screamed.

Malcolm reached out, grabbed her by the belt and yanked with all of his strength. He fell backwards and landed hard on his back on the sidewalk. She dropped her cup as she fell, landing on him and knocking the breath out of him. Her legs splayed in the air for a brief moment, then she tumbled to one side. Her phone skittered across the sidewalk and his book went flying.

Her coffee cup landed in front of the bus's tire, which crushed it and sprayed hot coffee into the crowd.

Malcolm was half-dazed from hitting the pavement so hard and from having a shapely but solidly built woman land on him. It was a moment before he recovered enough to realize that he was still holding her.

He let her go and she rolled away from him and got to her knees. Malcolm noticed that she had green eyes. She looked like she was about to say something, then the man that Malcolm had pegged as a lawyer reached down and helped her to her feet. Behind the two figures now standing above him, he saw that the bus had stopped; the bus driver was frantically running towards them. In the background, he heard people exclaiming about the near-accident and complaining about being splashed with coffee.

The middle-aged McDonald's lady walked up and handed the slightly battered cell phone to the brunette, and said, "Sweetie, you are one lucky girl."

The bus driver stepped on the book as he sped past Malcolm to get to his almost-victim. "Ma'am, are you all right?"

Malcolm sat up and considered the knot of people surrounding the woman he'd just rescued. He laboriously got to his feet.

"Yes, I'm fine. Just fine." She laughed. "Lost my coffee, though."

She had a nice laugh.

Malcolm picked up his book and took a last look at the crowd around the girl. He waved once and thought she saw him, then walked away, limping slightly.

6. MISSIONS

"So, who was she?" Malcolm asked, stopping to lean against the rough brick wall of a bank a few blocks from the intersection where he'd rescued the woman. "What was so special about her?"

He opened the book again.

> Her name is Lisa Hammond and she's a legal secretary for Fox, Kramer & Salzari. She's thirty-two years old, divorced, with a four-year-old son at home. She and her son are currently living with her mother.
>
> Lisa's future is in flux because some key factors must fall into place

for her to achieve her full potential. However, it's likely that she'll marry a prominent local doctor and, through him, become involved in volunteer work. Because of these activities, she'll discover that her organizational capabilities combined with her natural charm make her a formidable fundraiser for charities.

She'll do great things, and be an inspiration to others, if she's given the opportunity and the necessary encouragement.

It gave Malcolm a certain amount of satisfaction to think that she would do worthwhile things, because of him. He tried not to think about how good, how solid, she'd felt in his arms when he'd caught her. That just felt so...disloyal...to Ellen.

His stomach suddenly rumbled, which made him realize he was hungry. Really hungry. The book had sent him traipsing all around the waterfront area, so he'd really worked up an appetite. He'd skipped breakfast that morning, too, because eating a hearty meal before taking a terminal leap seemed pointless.

An image of his lifeless body floating in the river popped into his mind, then the hands of rescue workers reached down to pull him out of the gently undulating water. He shuddered slightly. Just because he wanted to be gone from the world, well, he was still a little uncomfortable with the whole idea of his dead body in the hands of anyone else, especially the cold, impersonal hands of the medical examiner.

He imagined the medical examiner walking into a waiting room (which looked suspiciously like the Visitor Lounge at Bayloft Memorial) where his brother, Jacob, had gathered his entire family. The examiner said, "I can assure you that it was over quickly."

His brother's scathing response: "What a loser!"

Even though it had been just a momentary fit of his imagination, that was just so like his ever-critical older brother. Malcolm shook his head, ruefully amused, and focused on the book again.

> **"If you're that hungry," said the book, "there's an excellent hot dog stand on Wister Street, right about where the Grange starts. It's in the direction we need to be going next anyway."**

Malcolm closed the book, pushed himself away from the wall and walked towards Wister Street, watching the buildings change from the standard business district norm to badly maintained and slightly dilapidated. He was familiar with the Grange, an area of a few blocks with lots of rickety booths and street vendors. Many types of goods were sold there: foods, handicrafts, knock-off clothing and purses, illegally ripped music and electronic devices of mysterious origin. All in all, a great place to find a bargain, especially if you were looking for a place with more of an edge than the local mall.

As he walked, Malcolm cracked the book open again to see what it had planned next.

Your next good deed is going to be a little different. Your target's name is Margaret Beachums. She's sixteen years old. She ran away from home when she was thirteen because her mother's boyfriend, Juan, kept molesting her and her alcoholic mother wouldn't believe her.

Her mother is Carol Bloom from Darlington, Missouri, and she's managed to clean up her act over the past three years. She kicked Juan loose long ago; he's in San Quentin over in California for twenty more years on unrelated charges (but he'll be shanked in prison in two years because he's got a big mouth). She's

gone back to her maiden name. She's straightened herself out with Alcoholics Anonymous, and spends a disproportionate amount of her time and money trying to track down her lost daughter. She still lives in the same old dump that she used to, but that's only because she's afraid to move in case her daughter ever tries to find her.

Margaret is going to die tonight from a bad batch of heroin unless you can convince her to go home to her mother. Margaret deserves a second chance at life. You're it.

You'll know her when you see her. Good luck.

Malcolm stopped in his tracks. He closed the book, then opened it again to the same page. The text still stopped halfway down the page. No new text had appeared.

This task wasn't just about being in the right place at the right time. This time, he had to interact with a junkie, and convince her to take an action that he was sure she wouldn't want to do. He flailed his arms and cursed loudly for a few moments, ignoring the uncomfortable stares and shocked glances from onlookers who skirted away from him as if he were a madman.

He didn't want to be responsible for the life of someone else. He had enough trouble with his own damn life.

When he calmed down, he realized he had the inklings of a plan. A crazy plan but, nevertheless, a plan. He went to the nearest ATM and took out eight hundred dollars, the maximum that his bank would let him withdraw in a single day. In his experience, money didn't buy happiness, but it was certainly a powerful lubricant if applied properly.

7. SECOND CHANCES

Malcolm folded the money in half, tucked it into a pocket and made his way to the Grange. He found the hot dog stand right where the book had indicated. He left the stand with two chilidogs, a Coke Zero and a wad of napkins. Good chilidogs were always messy, and these actually looked pretty good.

As he ate the first one, he looked around the area and studied the people. The crowd was ethnically diverse. If he had to guess, there were probably a hundred people within thirty yards of him. His target was probably one of them.

There were businessmen, housewives, lots of teenagers, would-be gangster types, skateboarders and more. OK, time to narrow things down. Anybody who wasn't a teenager could be eliminated. All the males, likewise.

Now, who did that leave?

As he scanned the crowd, he found only seven teenage girls that met his criteria. Well, a heroin addict would probably be thin, which narrowed it down a little further. Another thought struck him: How could a girl who'd left home at thirteen support herself for three years on the street and pay for a drug habit?

His eyes focused on a teenage girl who was standing by herself. Malcolm considered the lone girl a little more carefully and began walking in that direction. She was leaning against a building and was wearing a black mini-skirt, high heels and a low-cut yellow blouse. Even from this distance, Malcolm could see that she was painfully thin.

As he approached, he saw her exchange some words with a passing man. After a moment, the man shook his head and walked on.

Malcolm stopped in front of the girl and took a sip of his Coke Zero. She looked at him with raccoon eyes, which was how he thought of the cosmetics style where women put lots of dark makeup around their eyes.

"You lookin' for something?" The girl put her hand on her hip, cocked her elbow and flipped her long, black hair over her left shoulder.

"Maybe."

The girl looked around; nobody was close enough to hear them. She leaned forward and asked, "You a cop?"

"No."

"Fifty bucks and I can take you to heaven. Hundred gets you half-and-half."

"Not what I'm looking for, Margaret."

"What are—" She stopped in mid-sentence, and started backing away when she realized he knew her name. "Who the hell are you?"

"I'm your fairy godfather," Malcolm said, biting into his second chilidog. He chewed for a moment, swallowed and added, "I'm here to give you a second chance at life."

"You're crazy! Get away from me!" she shouted.

"OK." Malcolm turned his back and ambled slowly away from her. About ten yards away, he sat down on the edge of stone wall that functioned as the outer edge of a built-in planter for an office building. The small dirt area behind him contained a stump and a couple of twisted brown things that might once have been flowers. Maybe.

He munched on his hot dog and waited.

It took a couple of minutes, but he was once again provided with proof that curiosity was the most powerful force in the universe, not gravity or the strong nuclear force, or whatever—high school physics was a long time ago.

Margaret stood in front of him, about five feet away, probably at what she considered a safe distance from a potentially volatile, unpredictable man. He looked up and studied her. She looked like she was poised to flee.

"How'd you know who I am?" she asked.

"I'm your fairy godfather. I'm supposed to know these things." He smiled at her. "I mean, can you imagine your fairy godfather walking up and saying, '*Hey you, I'm gonna change your life*'?"

She giggled slightly. Well, that was something, at least.

"No really, how'd you know? Are you a private detective?"

"I'm not a detective."

"Did my Mom send you?"

"No, I've never met her." He took a sip from his can. "Although, it might interest you to know that she goes by Carol Bloom now. She went back to her maiden name."

"What happened to…?"

Malcolm shook his head. "Juan? He's long gone. He's doing a long stretch in prison in California. He's probably going to die in prison too. Especially if he doesn't keep his mouth shut."

"Yeah, he was always mouthin' off." She paused for a moment, as if looking off into the distance. Malcolm had heard that sort of expression described as a thousand-yard stare, an expression far too world-weary for the young face that was carrying it. "How do you know all this?"

"It's part of my job, you know, being a fairy godfather and all."

She put both of her hands on her hips and glared down at him. "I don't believe any of this. Especially that godfather thing."

"Fairy godfather, please. The 'godfather' thing is a whole different gig."

"Whatever."

"Tell you what, we can discuss it when you get back." He reached into his pocket, peeled a single bill off the wad, pulled it out and offered it to her. "I could use some fries. And get yourself whatever you want, too. Whatever's left, you can keep."

"I'm not hungry."

"Yes, you are. It's been long enough since your last fix, you should be feeling at least a little appetite. You need to keep your strength up."

She just looked at him for a long moment. "How do you know I'll come back?"

"I don't," Malcolm said. "On the other hand, how bad do you want answers?" He grinned at her.

He was unsurprised, but nevertheless pleased, when she returned about five minutes later. He'd rather pointedly made it clear that he wasn't watching her by, basically, looking in every direction except where she was.

She sat next to him this time, but about a foot away. She really was thin; her arm was white with painfully visible tendons and veins as she handed him a cardboard container with boardwalk-style fries. She'd gotten a cheeseburger, a bag of gummy bears and a Coke for herself. He waited for her to say something.

"That fairy godfather thing is lame, you know."

"Is it?" He ate a few fries. "I think it's pretty cool. I like fairy tales. I like believing that there's magic in the world." He washed the fries down with another swallow of his beverage. "Don't you?"

She snorted. "I ain't seen no magic."

"I thought so, too. And then I got my magic book, and everything was different. I mean, it's not like I set out to be a fairy godfather."

"Magic book?"

"Yes. Full of everything I need to know, when I need to know it, in order to do the job."

"You got a magic book?"

"Yes." Uh oh, he had a bad feeling. Maybe he shouldn't have mentioned the book.

"I don't believe you. If you've got a magic book, I dare you to show it to me."

Malcolm wasn't sure what to do. He had a magic book, apparently, but not the one he'd described to her. Not exactly. So he did what employees have done through the ages. He passed the buck.

He pulled the book out of his coat pocket and showed it to her. He was only half-way surprised to see that it was still just as dog-eared as before, but the cover was no longer the garish mash-up it had been. It now featured an abstract blue design with white lettering, and the title was:

The Fairy Godperson's Handbook
A Practical Framework for Proper Magical Wish Fulfillment

Margaret's mouth dropped open, then she laughed. "You can't be serious. That's not even possible."

She reached for the book, but Malcolm pulled it back. "Tsk, tsk," he said. "Would you just reach out and touch Harry Potter's wand if he were standing in front of you?" He thought about what he'd said for a couple seconds, then added, "Don't even go there."

Margaret giggled. He couldn't help it, and started laughing himself.

"In all seriousness, Margaret, losing you was the worst thing that ever happened to your mother. She turned her life around, joined AA, the whole works. And she still searches for you."

Margaret's smile hardened. "Where was she when I needed her? She never believed me, not once."

"What can I say? People make mistakes. Mix in alcohol…" He turned to look in her eyes. "Or heroin…and the mistakes get larger."

"Yeah, right."

"Did I tell you about the beautiful new house your mother lives in?"

"No."

"That's because she doesn't. She lives in the same crappy dump you both used to live in, even though she hates the house. And the memories. And the constant reminder of what a worthless mother she was. Do you know why she still lives there?"

Margaret was silent, looking at him with wide eyes. "No."

"Because she's afraid that someday you'll need her, and if she moves…you won't be able to find her."

"I didn't know," she said.

"No way you could know, not without a fairy godfather." Malcolm shrugged. "Now, I'd like you to cast your mind back to one time in your life when you were happy. Do you have something in mind?"

She just looked at him. He thought for a moment that he'd pushed her too hard. He half expected her to just get up and walk away. The silence stretched out uncomfortably.

"Yeah," she said, finally. "I was ten, and I was playing with Mom's makeup, looking in the mirror, just havin' a time, you know."

"OK. I want you to be that girl for a minute. Can you do that?" He waited until she nodded.

"All right. Would that girl want you to be where you are now?"

"No," she whispered.

"The thing about fairy tales is that they always come down to a choice. As your fairy godfather, I'm authorized to give you a second chance, but it's your decision what you do with it. Are you ready for your choice?"

"No."

"Sorry, life doesn't work like that." He took a sip of his Coke Zero, deliberately drawing out the suspense. "The girl you were, the one from the happy time…I want you to think hard about what she would want for herself. What she'd want for you. Can you do that?"

"I don't know…"

"On the one hand, you can treat this as just a random meeting with some delusional crackpot, and go on with your life as it is. You'll die tonight, but your mother will eventually be notified, so at least she'll know what happened to you. She'll have closure. Or you can go home. It's your choice."

"That's…that's crazy."

"Welcome to the world of magic." He reached into his pocket, pulled out the wad of money and held it out to her. "If you want to live, you take this money, you get a taxi to the bus station, and you get on a bus to Missouri."

She took the money from his hand. "How do you know I won't just take the money and run?"

"I don't. It's your choice to make, not mine." He stood up and stuck his arm in the air. A yellow taxi glided to a halt next to them. "Your ride's here."

Malcolm watched as Margaret got into the vehicle, then watched the taxi recede into the distance. He turned and walked down the street, wondering if he'd ever know whether he'd succeeded in changing her destiny.

8. APPENDIX F

Malcolm walked slowly back toward the waterfront and finally settled on a bench in McPherson Square, enjoying the warm breeze and the slanting afternoon sun shining on his face.

"Have you ever failed?" he asked, and opened the book once more.

> **"Yes, Malcolm. Probability does not equal actual outcome, otherwise it would be certainty. Free will trumps everything. So, yes, even magic books can fail. We all carry our scars, even magical books. My failures are listed in Appendix F, if you'd care to look."**

"Did I help Margaret?"

"She didn't take the taxi to the train station."

"I didn't really expect her to," Malcolm said, crossing his legs and leaning back. "Sometimes you have to hit rock-bottom before you can make changes in your life. She's not quite there yet. But now she knows she has an option she didn't have before."

"Her future is still uncertain."

"Life is uncertain, isn't it? I mean, I could get hit by a bus crossing the street. Did I at least improve her odds?"

"Yes. Margaret and her boyfriend were both going to die tonight. Now, Margaret might have a chance."

"So you're not trying to save the boyfriend?"

"There's a term you should be familiar with. *Triage.* I can't find any probability line where the boyfriend lasts more than another year, and mostly he causes harm to all those around him before he goes. Even magic has limits."

There was something vaguely unsettling, maybe disappointing, about that. First, he'd discovered that magic existed. Then he'd learned that magic wasn't "Abracadabra!" and everything is fixed, hey look, your wife and kids are just around the corner, they didn't die after all, it was just a bad dream. And now his vaunted magic book used the word "triage," which basically translated into a brutal conservation of resources to save…what?…only the most worthy?

Malcolm leaned back against the bench and tried to relax. He rolled his shoulders and opened his hands, which he'd unknowingly clenched into fists.

There was no need to get upset. He had free will and he was going to use it, by damn. He was proud to have done some good deeds today, but he was still destined for **Appendix F**, and that was all there was to it. This would all be over for him soon.

He asked, "So, how am I going to die? What's the plan?"

> **"Our deal was that you'd be 'provided with the opportunity to die a heroic death.' You were supposed to jump in front of the bus to save Lisa Hammond. That was going to be your heroic death."**

"What?" Malcolm found himself standing up, still holding the book. "But...but you didn't tell me that."

"Our deal didn't say anything about telling you when your opportunity arrived."

9. ROCK-BOTTOM

Driven by his rage, Malcolm walked all the way back to Donahoe Park. All the while, he'd felt his anger at the book growing by leaps and bounds. From street level, he trudged down the same concrete stairs that Beatrice McDonald had fallen from earlier in the day. *God, was it only this morning?*

He reached the asphalt circle at the bottom of the stairway. The fountain in the center of the circle was splashing in a soothing rhythm that Malcolm found somehow irritating—he didn't want to be soothed. The slanting rays of the afternoon sun glinted off the ripples generated by the fountain.

Hardesty Bridge loomed on the other side of the park from him. He could practically feel the long stairway up to the bridge level beckoning him. *Just a little further, and your pain will be gone.*

With his goal in sight, he believed that he deserved some answers.

"You lied to me," he said, pacing around the fountain and angrily flipping the book open.

"I didn't lie to you," the book said. "I promised you that you could have a hero's death rather than an ignomin- ious leap to your death from the bridge. It's not my fault you didn't seize the opportunity when it was provided to you."

"You bastard!" Malcolm shouted. "I did all this so I could die as hero!"

His outburst startled a female jogger who was passing through the circle; she gave him a wide-eyed glance and a wide berth as she huffed by.

"Malcolm, dying has nothing to do with whether you're a hero. You've saved two lives today, and maybe a third depending on what Margaret does. By every definition there is, you are a hero."

His voice shaking, Malcolm said, "That was your doing."

"I just provided information," the book said. "You saved them, not me. I'm just a book. Why did you rescue them?"

"Because I couldn't just let them get hurt," Malcolm said. "Not when I could save them."

"That's usually my line. This is what I do."
"Why them? What makes them so special?"
"Malcolm, I wasn't saving them. I was saving you."
"What?"
"You're the special one."

"I'm not special," Malcolm whispered, lowering the book.

He sat down on one of the benches spaced at intervals around the circle. He'd had a good life. He'd been happy. He wanted that life back. He wanted Ellen, and the children. He wanted to stop hurting.

He thought about getting up, climbing that staircase and just finishing it, maybe taking the book on the plunge with him since he was so angry at it. But he couldn't make himself get up off the bench.

Truthfully, he felt exhausted. Physically, and emotionally—just completely drained.

Malcolm started crying, the tears running down his cheeks. He hunched over as he started sobbing uncontrollably.

He heard a male voice say in disgusted tone, "Christ, man up, dude!" but a moment later a hand patted him on the back and a feminine voice said, "It'll be all right. Just let it all out. You'll feel better for it." The woman pressed a couple of napkins into his hand, then he heard the clicking of her high heels as she walked away.

Eventually he stopped sobbing, like the calm that slowly comes on after a violent thunderstorm. He wiped his eyes with the back of his hands, blew his nose with the napkins he'd been given.

Finally, he was ready to open the book again.

"Sometimes you have to hit rock-bottom before you can make changes in your life. Are you there yet?"

"You're brutal, aren't you?" he whispered. The book was using his own words to Margaret Beachums against him.

"Whatever it takes, Malcolm."

"You still lied to me."

"No. I've never lied to you. I told you what you needed to know, when you needed to know it."

"But it hurts so much."

"That's life. Joy and pain. Love and death. You can't have the good without the bad. But the good things, you hold on to them. You remember. Stop locking yourself away from world and wallowing in your own pain and loss."

"You're just lucky I didn't decide to jump off the bridge with you."

"Worse things have happened to me, Malcolm. I'm a little bit more durable than the average paperback. I've been every shape of book imaginable—a scroll, a modern book, a graphic novel, a video game a couple times. I was even a stone tablet, once."

"I planned this for so long," Malcolm said. "All I wanted to do was die."

"It's funny, in a way. As a doctor, you know so much more about the grieving process than most people. But you used your knowledge to subvert your own healing. You never let yourself recover. Somebody who really, really wanted to commit suicide would never have let me distract them from their purpose today."

"I miss them so much."

"And you'll remember them, forever and ever. But, Malcolm, you have the potential to touch more lives than anyone you've rescued today. Don't you really think that helping others is what Ellen would want you to do with the rest of your life?"

"Yes," Malcolm said.

"My job here is done. Just leave me on the bench. You should walk up Cannery Street on your way back to your car."

"After all we've been through together, you're just going to leave me for someone else?"

"That's basically the way it works."

"Good," Malcolm said. "Do you have any idea how tired I am? I don't think I could do another day like this."

Malcolm put the book down on the bench and stood up. He looked up at the Hardesty Bridge, then turned his back to it and walked away.

10. EPILOGUE

Malcolm walked up Cannery Street, limping a little from the day's exertions. He heard a woman's voice shout "Hey, you!" but he didn't think much of it. He was wondering whether his car had been towed, or booted, since he'd parked it in a two-hour parking zone in the morning, almost eleven hours ago.

He stopped and turned, though, when the voice shouted again and he heard high heels running after him. He turned and saw Lisa Hammond approaching.

"Hey," she said breathlessly when she reached him. "I thought I recognized you. With all the people around earlier, I never had a chance to thank you for saving my life."

Malcolm smiled. "No problem. I was just in the right place at the right time."

"No, you were awesome! I saw that bus comin' and I thought I was a goner," she said. "I'm Lisa Hammond, by the way." She grinned at him. "Hey, can I maybe buy you a coffee?"

He was nonplussed for a minute. Lisa wasn't conventionally pretty, but when she smiled it was like turning on a thousand-watt bulb.

"It's OK," she said, looking a little disappointed. "You don't have to if you don't want to."

"Yes, I'd love a cup of coffee. You just startled me a little." Malcolm laughed. "It's been a while since I've been…out and about like this. I'm Malcolm Jameson."

He held out his hand for her to shake, but she surprised him by cocking her arm pointedly. He linked his arm with hers and she led him down the street.

"How come you're limping?" Lisa asked.

"Because a gorgeous woman jumped on me this afternoon."

"So, you think I'm gorgeous?"

"I never said it was you. This happens to me all the time."

She mock-punched him in the arm and they both started laughing.

More than an hour later, Malcolm left the coffee shop, escorting Lisa to the local Metro stop. She'd insisted that they exchange phone numbers, and threatened to hunt him down if he didn't call her. He'd just stood there for a few long minutes after she'd gone through the gates.

Lisa was so much different than Ellen, and he couldn't help still feeling a twinge of guilt at having coffee with her. But she felt like a breath of fresh air in his life, and if that was a bit of a cliche, well, it was still true.

He turned when he felt someone unexpectedly tap his shoulder. It was a businesswoman, perhaps in her late twenties, wearing a sharply tailored business outfit. He'd never seen her before.

"Are you Malcolm Jameson?"

"Yes."

She was clearly nervous, twisting a lock of her hair with one hand. He looked down and saw that her other hand was holding a book, although he couldn't read the title. He brought his gaze back up to her face.

"I'm supposed to tell you that she got on the bus."

"Really?" Malcolm beamed at her. "That's great news. But what made her change her mind?"

"She went shopping and spent a bunch of the money you gave her, so she was late getting home.

Her boyfriend started the party without her, only he had a bad batch of heroin. He was dead so fast the needle was still sticking out of his arm when she found him." The woman stared at him with wide eyes, as if reluctant to say anything else.

"You helped her, didn't you?"

"Yeah, she came running down the stairs and I put her in the taxi I'd already called for her. I...I...told her I was her fairy godmother and she started crying, but she got in the taxi and she took it to the bus terminal."

"Good job," Malcolm said, and gave the woman a quick hug.

The woman looked around, as if scared that somebody would overhear her. "Is this real? Or am I going crazy?"

Malcolm laughed. "That book is pure magic." He walked away; he could practically feel her staring after him.

A little while later, he found his car parked on the side street where he'd left it in the morning. Wonder of wonders, it hadn't been towed or booted, but there was a folded-up note on the windshield. He picked up the note, unfolded it and read:

THIS IS <u>YOUR</u> LUCKY DAY!

EVERY DAY, WE PICK PARKING SPOTS
AT RANDOM
AND
WE PAY THE PARKING FEES FOR THE
DAY!!!!
THE WHOLE DAY!!!!!!!!!!!!!

— Citizens for a Better Downtown Experience —

Malcolm laughed so hard he had to lean over the car's hood to catch his breath.

It was a good day to be alive.

Did You Like This Book?

Please let everyone know by posting a review on Amazon, Goodreads or your favorite online retailer. Reviews are vital for authors, especially indie-published authors like me.

And don't forget…

I've got a bunch of **Extras** for you on the following pages.

EXTRAS

Afterward

The Afterward from the First Edition of the story, which was originally entitled *The Good Book*.

Behind the Scenes, Second Edition

Like the Director Commentary on a DVD, find out how the Second Edition of this story came to be created.

PREVIEW: The Whispering Voice

Check out this excerpt of *The Whispering Voice*, David Keener's next thrilling publication: a crime story, with just a touch of magic.

Afterward

The genesis of *An Unlikely Hero* came out of two driving imperatives.

First, there was this idea that wouldn't go away. Now, ideas are funny things. Some of them are elusive, fading away like soap bubbles in the wind almost before you can register them. But some ideas don't go away. They keep nagging at you until you do something with them.

My idea involved a magic book that would change somebody's life, which by itself isn't a particularly unique idea. But I didn't want the book to be some kind of static artifact or convenient McGuffin…I wanted it to be a character in and of itself. I wanted it to have a bit of attitude. In fact, I wanted the magic book to be so integral to the story that the plot would collapse without it, like Sherlock Holmes without Watson or *The War of the Worlds* without any Martian invaders.

It seemed to me that my refinements made the idea even more intriguing. At least to me and, hopefully, to readers.

Second, I like challenging myself. In life in general, but especially in writing, I've found that I improve the most when I push my own boundaries. Generally, my stories are crime or mystery stories set in fantasy or science fiction backgrounds, often with a certain degree of fast-paced action and violence.

This magic book story, though, clearly wasn't that type of story.

I envisioned an emotional story with some heart-wrenching moments, hopefully leavened with a bit of humor. It would be set in our everyday world. No guns, no bloodshed, no murders…with just the touch of magic embodied in the magic book.

As with any story, my main character had to have something at stake. The opening scene almost wrote itself. A man is ready to jump off a bridge, prevented only by a random bicyclist who stops and hands him a mysterious book.

Of course, I researched my story, as I do with any story. Simply Google "suicide bridge" and you'll see pictures of bridges all over the world with utterly ridiculous death tolls. It's common enough that one anonymous pundit made the truly horrifying quip: "If you build it high enough, they will jump."

In *An Unlikely Hero*, Malcolm Jameson is depressed, true, but he's essentially talked out of suicide by the magic book. In my story, he's *reachable*. In real life, there are people who are so far down that they can't even conceive of a way out. Often, they don't even have anybody in their life that understands how far gone they are, and nobody to get them the help that they need.

Malcolm learns that he's connected to so many other people just by the things he does, or can do in the future. So are you.

If you can make a difference in somebody's life…make that difference. If this story inspires just one person to do that, well, that'd be a truly fine thing.

David Keener
October 22, 2016
Ashburn, Virginia

BEHIND THE SCENES, SECOND EDITION

This story was originally published under the title, *The Good Book*. I knew, of course, that the title had biblical connotations, but at the time I published it there were literally no instances of books published on Amazon with that phrase in the title. And it was a descriptive title, because the story is literally about a magic book trying to do good things.

Yeah, well, sales were dismal.

The interesting thing was that the people who did read the story really liked it.

I know this, because some of them contacted me to tell me how much it meant to them. The most heart-wrenching one was this one I received in October of 2017:

David:

Today would have been my 47th wedding anniversary. Ruth died two and a half years ago after a series of strokes over seven years. My eldest daughter died on the 22nd of October in 1992.

I have not laughed so hard as when the book changed to be a handbook for Fairy do gooders. It was a roll-on-the-floor laughing moment.

I found the story a few days ago on Amazon and read it this evening.

Obviously there is magic in the world.

Thanks,

Charles

It's immensely gratifying to know that, despite everything, you've connected with a reader, and that you've somehow made their day just a little bit better. It's like a form of magic all by itself. An idea, a story, had moved from my head to another person…and they'd understood, and appreciated, what I'd been trying to accomplish.

That makes up for a lot of things.

And it told me that that the story worked, that it was doing what it was supposed to.

The failure was in my marketing. My fault.

Stepping back and really evaluating the story, it was essentially a story about redemption, with just a touch of magic and, perhaps, a hint of humor.

Nothing about the marketing really said that. The title didn't communicate that. And, well, neither did the cover.

The cover…was another of my mistakes.

I'd tried out several different covers on people who had read the story. They all chose the gray cover with the fog-enshrouded bridge (see the next page), because it really resonated with them.

Well, it didn't resonate with people who *hadn't* read the story. Literally. With lots of vibrant cover thumbnails on Amazon, nobody, but nobody, clicked on the thumbnail for *The Good Book*. And you can't sell a book if people aren't even looking at it.

I gradually and reluctantly came to the conclusion that if I ever expected the story to generate any sales, it was going to need a second edition that corrected some of its marketing issues.

This was underscored when I participated in a panel at Capclave 2018 in Rockville, MD. Capclave is a long-running literary convention focused on the science fiction and fantasy genres. The panel was "Blurred Lines: Writing and Marketing Mixed Genre Books."

Clearly, *The Good Book* was a mixed-genre book, combining the real world with a bit of fantasy and some metaphysical leanings. After I brought up my marketing woes, we ended up discussing the book as an example of how *not* to market such a book. You might think that I'd have been upset about this, but I wasn't.

Even though I'd never intended to be the case study for the session, my fellow panelists and the audience were both sympathetic and exceedingly helpful.

To show that I'm not a complete and utter slouch at marketing, I held up a copy of my book and told the audience that they should buy a copy of the first edition because it was going out of print very soon and would thus become a collector's edition.

Not only did this elicit a wave of laughter, but several audience members approached me afterward to buy copies. I sold out of all my remaining print copies at the convention.

And now here we are.

You're reading the second edition, which largely exists because of that panel. The story hasn't changed, but everything else has. I still believe in the story. I hope you feel the same.

David Keener
October 3, 2018
Ashburn, Virginia

PREVIEW

THE WHISPERING VOICE

Turn the page for an excerpt from *The Whispering Voice*, the next thrilling story from David Keener.

In Philadelphia, a woman comes into a bar with a deadly problem…and gets far more help than she expected. Because this isn't just any bar. It's a magic bar that appears at different times throughout history, presided over by the legendary Gilgamesh, who has been cursed to witness history from its confines but to never leave.

THE WHISPERING VOICE
Chapter 1 Preview

What she needed more than anything was a drink.

Anna Brodie knew it was wrong, knew that alcohol was the furthest thing from what she really needed, but old, old habits died hard. A drink, just one drink, and then she'd leave and do what needed to be done.

Liquid courage.

Driving down Frankford Avenue in her Toyota Camry, it was easy to convince herself that—she glanced over at the radio/clock to see the time—at 11:17 AM on a fine, sunny Monday morning, the best thing she could do in her situation was to walk into a bar. Yeah, right. And then reality obliged her; there was a new bar up ahead where Linda's Cafe had been before it went out of business. The only thing that was odd was that it didn't have a neon sign like most of the other businesses around it, just a wooden sign with a design that seemed vaguely Mesopotamian.

She slowed down, turned right and followed a narrow lane to the parking lot behind the bar.

Walking back down the lane to get to the bar's front entrance, she had to move to one side as an old, battered sedan with more rust than paint rolled slowly past her toward the lot in back. The driver, a twenty-something man with long, lanky hair and a sallow face, gave her a lingering once-over as he went by. The way he looked at her made her feel dirty, like an object and not a woman. She was probably almost twice his age, with a daughter and a husband waiting for her back home.

Waiting for her...and here she was, about to walk into a bar for the first time in eighteen years. Anna almost turned around, but then she realized that she'd have to face the man in the car again. A moment later, she was around the corner and pushing her way into the bar. It was dim inside, with a few rough-hewn wooden tables scattered around and a bar with five or six mismatched stools directly opposite the entrance. The establishment was empty, except for a lone customer at the bar.

Approaching, she saw that her fellow customer was a man in what looked like a long, dark robe with the hood pulled up so that it obscured his face. That was weird, kind of gangsterish in a way, and not really something she recalled seeing in any bar except maybe around Halloween. Still, he didn't worry her the way the man in the car had.

She took a seat a couple places down from the robed man. Then the bartender came out of the back and drove any thoughts of her fellow morning drinker out of her head. He was tall, a head taller even than her husband, who'd once played college football, and broad-shouldered like he could wrestle a bull to the ground with his bare hands. She shook her head. She had no idea why that image had popped into her head.

Coming over, he said, "Name's Gil. What would you like?"

"Shot of tequila."

"Don't have tequila."

She frowned. What kind of bar didn't have tequila? "A shot of anything, then."

He looked at her inscrutably. "All right."

The bartender turned around and pulled what looked like a ceramic jar off a shelf. Not even a bottle, a jar. She didn't know of any alcoholic beverages that came in ceramic packaging. Still, it looked clear and dangerous when he poured a measure into the shot glass he'd placed in front of her.

Behind her, she heard somebody come into the bar, though she was too busy contemplating the drink in front of her to turn and see who'd walked in. Besides, if it was the man from the parking lot, somehow she wasn't the least bit worried with Gil here. She barely noticed as the bartender walked away.

"You going to drink that or just look at it?" The voice came from the man sitting a few seats down the bar from her. She glanced sideways, but still couldn't see his face because of the hood.

"Drink it," she answered. "At least, I think so."

"Trying to work up your courage, eh?"

"Yeah."

"I know how it is," the man said. "You've got a problem you can't figure out how to solve. So you reach for the thing that will at least make you feel better." The man turned towards her and pulled back his hood. He had penetrating blue eyes, an olive complexion, a roughly trimmed red beard and what looked like an afro that was just as red as his beard. Whatever ethnicity he was, she'd never beheld the combination before. "Except that you know that it won't really make you feel better. And it won't solve your problem, either."

Anna couldn't help it. The tears started flowing. In a moment, she was hunched over her shot glass, shoulders shaking with the force of her sobs. As she cried, she was dimly aware that the man had moved to the stool next to her and was rubbing her back in a comfortable, fatherly way, while calmly telling her that everything was going to be fine.

She looked up at him through her tears. "You don't know a thing about my situation."

The man shrugged and gave her a quirky smile. "How long have you been sober?"

"What?"

"It's a simple question. I know you know the answer."

She sighed. "My last drink was eighteen years, ten months and twenty days ago." Since she'd found out she was pregnant with her daughter and realized that her totally out-of-control lifestyle of parties, alcohol and nose candy had to end.

"You can call me Khalish," the man said. "I'm afraid you'd find my full name terribly difficult to pronounce." He looked down at her shot glass. "Offer me your drink."

Anna tilted her head and looked at him for a moment. He had blue eyes in a weathered face that made it hard to guess his age, although he certainly wasn't young. There was a strange intensity to his gaze, as if her offering the drink to him was somehow important in a way that she didn't understand. She pushed the shot glass in his direction, though her emotions were in such a whirl that she couldn't have said precisely why she did it. Except that, somehow, she trusted Khalish.

He smiled and reached up to gently cup her cheek in his hand. "Go clean yourself up, Anna. When you come back, you can tell me about your problem."

Anna nodded, unable to speak, suddenly hopeful that maybe there was a way out of her situation. A way for her husband and daughter to survive the catastrophe that had befallen them. It didn't occur to her to wonder how Khalish knew her name.

After Anna left to find the bar's facilities, such as they were, Khalish crooked his finger and beckoned the bartender over.

"I see you tricked your way into getting a drink," Gil said.

"It's not trickery," Khalish answered. "She gave me an offering. She needs our help."

Gil raised his eyebrows. "Our help?"

"Yours, really," Khalish admitted. "At least right now."

"How do they say it nowadays?" The bartender pretended to think for a moment. "Yes, I remember now. Screw you. I don't do the bidding of the gods, not even a minor has-been like you."

Khalish laughed. "Don't get uppity with the gods, Gilgamesh. It didn't work out so well for you last time."

Gil leaned over the bar, which might have been intimidating to most people, but intimidation emphatically didn't work on Khalish. As divine beings went, he was barely on the scale, but if intimidation had an opposite, opposing force, he basically embodied it.

"Gil," he whispered. "The man at the table by the door has been trailing Anna to make sure she follows the instructions she's been given. Since she hasn't, he's going to kill her as soon as she leaves. I admit, you don't have to do anything I tell you, but if you don't take him out, her blood will be on your hands, not mine."

"Why don't you do it, then?"

Khalish sighed. "I'd be happy to. The man's a murderer, a rapist and robber. But I'm bound to influence, not to intervene directly. It's better this way. We really don't need another fiasco like Pompeii." He shook his head. "Just help her, Gil. Please."

ABOUT THE AUTHOR

In the cupola of the International Space Station.

David Keener is an author, editor and public speaker who lives in Northern Virginia with his wife and two (oops, three) inordinately large dogs. He writes science fiction, fantasy and mystery but loves the idea of mashing up his favorite genres in new and (hopefully) unexpected ways.

He is the grand instigator behind the *Worlds Enough* anthology series, and co-editor of the first volume, *Fantastic Defenders*. His next anthology will be *The Forever Inn*, about a mysterious inn that travels randomly throughout the multiverse.

He frequently speaks at conventions (well, he did before COVID-19 happened, anyway), where he often conducts writing workshops. Find out more about him at:

Website: http://www.davidkeener.org
FaceBook: DavidKeenerWrites
Twitter: @keenersaurus

ACKNOWLEDGMENTS

It takes a village to help a wannabe writer become a published writer. For this, my first published story of non-trivial length, a whole bunch of people helped out, including: Debby Allen, Don Anderson, Mike Bresner, John Dwight, Angela Felsted, Cherlyn Guinyard, Elizabeth Hayes, Jeffrey Jacobs, Susan Jordan (RIP), Sally Keener, Jerry Moore, Michael Raymond, Donna Royston and Beth Sadler.

Rob a Bank, or Else...

Anna would never rob a bank, but now she has two hours...or her family dies. Even the police can't help her. When she stops at a bar for a shot of liquid courage and a little time to think through her options, she gets far more than she bargained for...because this isn't just any bar.

It's the Ur-Bar, a mysterious establishment that has appeared in different locations throughout history. A place where the walls between reality and fantasy are thinner than a scream.

And if there's magic left in the world, this is where Anna will find it...

IMAGE CREDITS